Paddy T. and the Time-Travelling Trampoline

ADAM FRANCE   ILLUSTRATED BY ZAHRA ZAINAL

ALLEN&UNWIN
SYDNEY·MELBOURNE·AUCKLAND·LONDON

First published by Allen & Unwin in 2019

Allen & Unwin
83 Alexander Street
Crows Nest NSW 2065
Australia
Phone: (61 2) 8425 0100
Email: info@allenandunwin.com
Web: www.allenandunwin.com

 A catalogue record for this
book is available from the
National Library of Australia

ISBN 978 1 76052 376 3

For teaching resources, explore
www.allenandunwin.com/resources/for-teachers

Cover design by Sandra Nobes
Text design by Evi-O Designs & Sandra Nobes
Set in 12 pt GT Super Text by Midland Typesetters & Sandra Nobes
Printed in Australia in September 2019 by McPherson's Printing Group

10 9 8 7 6 5 4 3 2 1

The paper in this book is FSC® certified.
FSC® promotes environmentally responsible,
socially beneficial and economically viable
management of the world's forests.

Contents

For the France family –
thank you for being unpredictable

The Trampoline

Troy reached the window and smacked it hard.

'Too easy,' he announced as he came crashing back down to earth. 'I can do that with my eyes closed.'

Troy and I had been given a trampoline for Christmas. Not a normal trampoline with protective netting and plastic piping as springs. No, Mum and Dad brought an ancient one home from a garage sale. Old biting springs. Giant rusty metal rails.

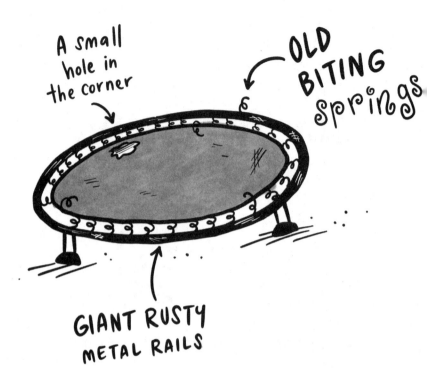

A small
hole in
the corner

OLD
BITING
springs

GIANT RUSTY
METAL RAILS

A small hole in the corner of the mat. I guess it was cheaper than the iPad Troy and I had been begging for.

Just to prove how little Dad cared about safety, he let us set it up on the cement slab out the back. As long as we weren't inside fighting over the PlayStation, he didn't care.

Mum, on the other hand, tried to reassure herself by covering the rusty rails in bubble wrap. This lasted a whole hour before Troy and I popped all the bubbles.

Every jump came with a high-pitched squeak that had our 'new' neighbours slamming their windows shut.

Our 'new' neighbours weren't all that new. But no one who moves into that house ever lasts more than six months.

So we just call everyone who lives there our 'new' neighbours.

For the past three weeks, Troy and I had been competing to see who could jump higher. We set the trampoline up against the side of the house and used Dad's blue pool-cue chalk on our hands to mark our height.

Troy's blue handprint sat clean on our older sister Nina's upstairs window. She opened it up when she heard the commotion.

'Just stop it!' Nina yelled. 'It's so annoying!'

'*It's so annoying!*' Troy mimicked. 'At least we're still using our present.'

'Yeah, what happened to the mobile phone Mum and Dad bought you?' I chimed in.

3

Troy and I smirked. We already knew the answer.

'Didn't you know it isn't waterproof?'

We laughed. Nina gritted her teeth before slamming her window shut.

'All right.' I turned to my younger brother. 'You want a challenge?'

'Hit me,' Troy accepted.

I pointed to the roof. Troy shook his head.

'No, Paddy. We've tried this. It's impossible to reach the roof. We can't get enough spring.'

'I didn't say you have to *reach* the roof,' I began, crossing my arms. 'I challenge you to jump *from* it.'

4

Troy's eyes traced the side of the house all the way to the top. He scratched his head.

'You want me to jump from up there?' he asked uncertainly.

I nodded.

'That's, like, two storeys high,' he said. 'And the trampoline is on the cement. How do you know I won't fall through?'

I gave him a grin. He was right; it was a crazy idea. But I knew what it took to make him do it.

'Well, I guess you'll just have to find out. That's if you're not too chicken?'

Troy looked at me with furious eyes. He hated being called chicken.

'Where's Dad's ladder?'

Troy stood on top of the roof looking down at the trampoline.

'You ready?' I called out.

'Are you sure it will hold?' he asked, hesitating.

'Just do it!' I yelled.

Troy swallowed and stepped forward.

'Geronimo!' he screamed as he jumped from the roof. He came down in a blur of speed.

He hit the trampoline.

Then disappeared.

Gone. Nothing. Not even a squeak of the springs.

'Troy?' I called out. 'Where'd you go?'

Silence.

'Troy?' I repeated anxiously.

I started looking around, trying to find him. I even climbed the ladder and looked up on the roof, as if I had just imagined him jumping. Nothing.

I was so confused. I didn't know what to do. I was about to call out to Mum, but I knew she would never believe Troy had disappeared into thin air. Disappeared into a trampoline.

I had to find Troy myself. I had to disappear into the trampoline and find my little brother.

I looked up at the roof again. It was my only hope.

Standing at the edge of the roof, I now understood why Troy was worried about jumping. The trampoline looked so small against the cement ground. But this was no time to be afraid.

I took a deep breath and jumped. With my eyes set on the trampoline, I watched the black rectangle grow. Larger and larger. I braced myself for impact.

But I never hit the mat. Instead, I splashed into deep, dark water. So dark that I couldn't see a thing.

SPLASH!

Then I felt something grab my wrist and pull me up out of the blackness. I was met by blinding light. I shielded my eyes, blinking until everything came into focus.

I felt something grab my wrist &

≥ PULL ≤ me out of

the blackness

GRAB!

I looked around and noticed I was sitting on the trampoline. On the cement in my backyard. Pushed up against the side of the house. Everything looked normal. Except that, for some reason, Dad's ladder no longer stood against the side of the house.

I felt a tap on my shoulder.

'Paddy?'

I turned around. Sitting behind me on the trampoline was a man with a giant beard. As I looked closer, I realised this wasn't just some random person sitting beside me. It was Troy. An older, hairier version of my brother.

He chuckled, his beard bouncing on his face.

'You look ridiculous.' He laughed nervously, his voice deep. His eyes slightly anxious.

I jumped off the trampoline and ran for the downstairs window. I couldn't believe what I saw in the reflection there. I had a moustache. I had long hair. I had forehead wrinkles!

'What is going on?' I called out to my not-so-young younger brother.

He was **BIGGER.**

He had a **GIANT** beard

He was **OLDER.**

'The trampoline,' Troy answered. 'It must be a portal into our futures.'

'This can't be,' I said, stroking Troy's long beard. 'This is just a dream.'

Troy tugged on my moustache.

'Ouch!' I yelled out. 'What did you do that for?'

'I wanted to see if it was real.'

Just then, the window above opened. Out popped my sister's head. An older head. An adult head.

'Don't you two have jobs to go to or something?' she asked.

'Nina?' I asked.

'No, Paddy, it's Lady Gaga.'

A cry came from inside her room. A baby's cry. A cry different to my baby sister Bella's.

'Now look what you've done. You've woken Madison.'

Troy and I looked at each other in shock.

'Okay,' Troy finally said.

'Sorry,' I added.

Nina shook her head before returning inside and shutting the window.

Frozen in fear, Troy and I continued to stare at each other.

'This is too weird,' I said. 'We need to get back home.'

'But we *are* home,' Troy replied, his thick beard almost hiding his trembling lips.

I looked at him with horrified eyes. I could feel the wrinkles on my forehead move.

'No, Troy. I want to go back to being a kid again.'

Troy could hear the fear in my voice.

'All right,' he said as he turned and looked at the roof. 'Let's go find Dad's ladder.'

This was all too familiar, I thought as I stood on the edge of the roof looking down at the trampoline.

'You ready?' Troy asked.

All I could do was nod before we jumped together. We fell down towards the black mat. Faster and faster. I could feel my hair flying in the breeze. My moustache flicking my lips.

Then I hit the trampoline and entered dark water. This time, I swam to the surface myself. I let my eyes adjust to the light. The trampoline came into view. The cement. The house. Everything as it was before. All except the ladder.

'Oh no.'

A voice came from behind. I turned around. I couldn't believe what I was seeing. Sitting on the trampoline was a man. No hair. Grey beard. Wrinkly, spotty skin.

'Troy?' I asked in shock.

Troy leaned forward and plucked a hair from my ear.

'Ouch!' I yelled. 'That hurt!'

He held it up. It was as white as snow.

'Paddy,' he said, his eyes wide. 'We're old!'

The window above opened. Out poked a head. But it wasn't Nina's.

'Uncle Troy? Uncle Paddy, is everything okay?' the woman asked. 'Do you guys need me to bring down your walking sticks?'

Troy and I looked at each other.

'The ladder!' we both cried.

Our legs were too frail to stand on the roof. We sat on the edge looking down at the trampoline.

'This is it,' Troy said, rubbing his back. 'If things don't work out, it was nice to know you, brother.'

We leaned in to give each other a hug but lost our balance and fell off the roof. We tumbled out of control.

I closed my eyes as I hit the black water. I swam to the surface and felt the bright light behind my eyelids.

I slowly opened my eyes. The surroundings gradually came into view. The trampoline. The cement. The house. Dad's ladder.

I jumped off the trampoline and ran to the downstairs window. I looked at my reflection. The moustache was gone. No ear hairs. No wrinkles. I was staring back at me. Twelve-year-old Paddy Thompson.

'Yes!' I yelled out in relief.

I spun around to see if Troy was back to normal too.

But he wasn't there.

The window above opened. Nina poked her head out. The real Nina.

'How many times do I have to tell you to stop being so annoying?' she called out.

'At least a hundred!' a familiar voice shouted.

Nina and I both looked up to see nine-year-old Troy standing on the edge of the roof.

'Geronimo!'

Fishing on the 8th

'**Found one!**' I called as I reached down into the murky water and retrieved the golf ball from between my toes.

'How many's that?' Marty asked as he concentrated on what was beneath his feet on the other side of the pond.

I looked into my bucket and made a rough estimate.

'About twenty, I think.'

Marty returned a thumbs-up. Twenty golf balls was pretty good for half an hour. But we had to rush. The sun had reached the trees at the end of the fairway and soon we wouldn't be able to see a thing. Then we would go home and wash the balls in the laundry sink before selling them back to the golf club for fifty cents per ball. Easy money. But the only money we ever got.

You see, neither Marty nor I got pocket money. Our families didn't have a lot of money, so we were always finding creative ways to make our own. And this was one of the best ideas we'd ever had.

Marty and I had been coming to the golf course for about three months. We quickly learned that the swampy water at the bottom

of the 8th hole – in which we now stood –
was the 'Jackpot Pond'. We had collected
hundreds of golf balls from this spot. And
with all the money we'd made from reselling
the balls back to the club, Marty and I almost
had enough to buy the new drum kit for sale
at Top Hill Music. And with the old guitar
I got for my last birthday, we'd start a band.
Then all we'd need was a name.

'How about The Lemon Squeezes?' Marty
suggested.

I turned and gave him a sour expression.
He got the picture.

'Yeah, too cheesy,' Marty admitted.

'The Muddy Middletoes?' I said.

We both burst out laughing. We knew it
was a daggy name. But then again, most
band names are.

Darkness hit the water as the sun
continued to drop behind the hills, signalling
it was time for us to leave.

'Righto,' I announced, looking to the skies.
'Let's get these to the laundry.'

We both started to leave the water when I stumbled, and my foot became wedged between two rocks. I tried to wrench it free but the more I tried, the further it sank.

'I'm stuck!' I called as I reached down and attempted to pull my leg out. Nothing.

'Stop playing around,' Marty yelled from the other side of the pond. 'It's almost dark; let's go.'

I yanked at my foot again but the swampy mud only sucked it down further.

'I'm serious!' I screamed. 'And I think I'm sinking!'

Marty could see the horror on my face. He dropped his bucket of golf balls and ran back to the water.

'Quickly!' I screamed in desperation as my knee met the rocks.

Marty began to swim in my direction. His arms thrashed. His legs kicked frantically. He lifted his head to see how far he had left to swim.

And then he stopped. His wide eyes stared

at me before slowly moving upwards towards the sky.

'Don't stop!' I called out. 'I'm still sinking!'

But Marty didn't move. His gaze was still fixed on the sky. His face twisted in shock.

Then a shadow covered his face. And then his body.

I slowly turned my head around. My jaw dropped. My heart stopped. Standing above me was a giant serpent, rearing at least five metres above the water. Its bright yellow eyes were locked on mine. Its silvery blue body a tessellation of dinner-plate-sized scales. I was frozen in fear. I couldn't blink. I couldn't breathe.

And then it slowly lowered itself back into the water and disappeared.

I turned back towards Marty.

'Wh-where did it go?' he stammered, surveying the water.

'I – I don't know,' I choked out, searching the pond around me.

Everything was completely silent.

And then I felt the rocks around my knee fall away. A moment later, I was launched out of the water.

I thrashed for something to grab onto as I was lifted into the air, and realised when my fingers touched scales that I was on the back of the serpent's head.

I was too petrified to make a sound. Before I could believe what was happening, I was being slowly lowered towards the side of the pond. Then I slid from the giant snake's head and landed on my feet.

I stood there looking at the serpent's eyes. Something about the way it looked back made me feel calm and relaxed.

With the flick of its lime-green tongue, the creature returned to the water, sliding under the murky surface without making a ripple.

Stunned, Marty stood in the middle of the pond.

'What just happened?' he asked, his voice so high-pitched it was almost unrecognisable.

I looked down at my knee. Besides a few small scratches, it was all right.

'I think it just rescued me.'

Marty started to hurry out of the water but stopped near the edge.

'Found one.' He reached down between his toes. Then I saw his expression change.

He lifted something
from the water.
It wasn't a golf ball.

In Marty's hand
sat something bright
green. Covered in
black and blue
spots. The size
of a football.
And almost the
same shape.

Marty's eyes met
mine. It was like looking
into a mirror, our expressions full of shock as
we realised what the object must be: a serpent
egg.

The silence was broken by a small splash
on the other side of the pond. Marty and I
took off at lightning speed down the fairway.
We couldn't get away fast enough.

At last we stopped and collapsed to the
ground at the golf club entrance. As I caught
my breath, I looked over at Marty.

I couldn't believe what I was seeing. The serpent's egg was still clutched in his hands. Its colours glowed against his terrified face.

'What are you doing?' I asked in disbelief. 'Why are you still holding that thing?'

'I – I...' he stammered, unable to take his eyes off it. 'I don't know. I panicked. The noise. I just ran.'

'Put it away before someone sees it,' I demanded.

Marty quickly placed the egg inside the bucket.

I looked up at the clubhouse in the distance.

'We'll sort this out tomorrow.'

We both decided overnight that we were retired from fishing for golf balls. And as we waited outside the office of the Top Hill Golf Club manager, Mr Ridgeman, to sell him our last bucket of balls, we decided it was probably a good thing to let him know about the serpent in the pond and the egg inside the backpack Marty was currently wearing. Then he would be able to relocate them both somewhere far from the pond. And once we knew the pond was serpent-free, maybe, just maybe, we would come out of retirement.

'So you're trying to tell me there is a monster on my golf course?' Mr Ridgeman, counting the golf balls, chuckled at what he just heard.

'Well, I wouldn't call it a monster,' I corrected, trying to find the right words.

'It's like an anaconda,' Marty offered.

Mr Ridgeman looked up from the balls.

'Boys,' he said, eyeing us both off, 'does this look like the Amazon rainforest?'

His furrowed eyebrows and tight-lipped scowl suggested he wasn't amused anymore.

It was no use.

'You got us,' I lied. 'We were just trying to trick you.'

Marty looked over at me and motioned towards the backpack. I returned a quick shake of the head.

Marty looked back at Mr Ridgeman and nodded in agreement.

'April Fool!' he called out.

Mr Ridgeman rolled his eyes and continued to count the balls.

'That's twenty-four.' He reached into his top drawer and pulled out a pile of loose change and counted it on the desk. 'And here's twelve dollars.'

'Thanks, Mr Ridgeman.' I said as I pocketed the money.

'No problem, boys,' he said. But his eyes were stern. 'And let's not forget it's November, not April, gentlemen. So it's probably best to keep your fantasy stories about mythical creatures to yourselves.'

Marty gulped.

'Yes, Mr Ridgeman,' we said together.

We didn't wait for a goodbye. We turned and made our way out of the golf club.

'Wow.' Marty looked at the ground as he walked. 'Mr Ridgeman is a real jerk.'

The sun broke from behind the clouds and

I realised I had left my hat in Mr Ridgeman's office.

'Wait here, I won't be a second.' I jogged back towards the clubhouse.

Walking up the hallway towards Mr Ridgeman's office, I noticed his door was closed. I leaned in to knock, but I heard him speaking aggressively and waited.

'Yes, two boys!' he said. 'The pond behind the eighth green.'

He was talking about us. He was probably on the phone to my parents, telling them that I was a liar.

'They found the serpent. And now we know where it is.'

My heart stopped. I couldn't believe it: Mr Ridgeman knew about the creature. And he'd spoken to us like we were talking nonsense.

'Round up the team, George,' he continued from behind the door. 'Tomorrow morning we're going hunting.'

I gasped out loud. I tried to push it back in by covering my mouth, but it was too late.

'Hang on a second, George.'

There was no time. I ran and ducked behind two golf bags. Mr Ridgeman's head appeared in his doorway. He looked left and right before closing the door again.

I jumped up and ran as fast as I could out of the clubhouse. Marty hadn't moved. I ran straight past and motioned for him to follow.

'What's happening?' Marty asked as he caught up.

I stopped at the front entrance to the golf course. Marty and I dropped to the ground trying to catch our breath.

'Was the serpent in the clubhouse?' Marty asked, trying to make sense of my panicked run.

'No,' I replied between breaths. 'But as of tomorrow there won't be a serpent.'

Marty looked at me, confused.

'What do you mean?'

'Mr Ridgeman and some others are going to kill it.' I stood and looked at the clubhouse. 'And I can't let that happen.'

Marty stood beside me, following my stare towards Top Hill Golf Club. I could sense he felt the same.

It was time the rescued became the rescuer.

'How are we going to do it?' Marty asked.

I stood there for a moment before looking at the backpack.

'I have a plan.'

★ ★ ★

The sun had barely broken the horizon as I stood on the bank of Jackpot Pond.

'You think this will work?' Marty asked, staring at the swampy water from his dad's office chair.

'We'll soon find out.'

I gave Marty a nod and started frantically thrashing the water with my hands. Marty remained silent in the office chair that was roped to my bike on the grass nearby.

'Help! Help!' I screamed. I kicked and slapped the surface of the pond, the sound echoing across the golf course. 'I'm stuck! Help!'

As I continued to flail, I looked back at Marty, his face anxiously searching the water for a sign. Nothing.

'Come on!' I screamed at the pond. 'I know you're here!'

My arms and legs began to get tired. And with one final slap at the surface, I overbalanced and fell in.

'It's no use,' I called back to Marty. 'It doesn't care.'

'Paddy,' Marty replied.

'This was a silly idea,' I continued, ignoring him. 'There's no way we—'

'Paddy!' Marty interrupted loudly.

I sat up in the water and followed Marty's

horrified gaze to the pond behind me. And there it was, rising high above the water with its slick scales shimmering against the rising sun. Its head tilted. Its bright yellow eyes locked on my submerged body.

I was spotted. I didn't have much time. I only had one chance.

I slowly rose to my feet and backed out of the water, my eyes never leaving those of the serpent. Once back on the grass, I blindly reached down and found my bike.

'Okay, Marty,' I whispered. 'On the count of three.'

From the corner of my eye, I could see Marty give a slow nod.

'One.' I gently lifted the bike by the handlebars, my eyes still on the serpent's.

'Two.' I slowly backed the bike away from the pond's edge.

The serpent's green tongue began to flicker. Its bright yellow eyes blinked.

'Three!' I screamed as I jumped on the bike.

I looked across at Marty just in time to

see him hold the serpent egg high above his head.

'C-come get it!' he spluttered, his body visibly trembling with fear.

I started pedalling as fast as I could down the fairway before feeling the rope pull tight. As I raced forward, I heard an ear-piercing scream. I turned to see Marty holding desperately onto the speeding office chair at the end of the rope. The bright green egg sat firmly between his legs.

And then I saw the serpent. Its body slithering with intent towards Marty. Its tail

whipping against the grass. Its eyes narrowed on the egg.

'Faster, Paddy!' Marty yelled from behind.

I pushed harder and faster along the fairway. My legs burning. My heart racing. My eyes set on my destination: Two Trees Creek. It was now only a couple of hundred metres ahead. When we reached it, Marty would throw the egg in the water. And the serpent would follow. And it would be free to live in peace.

That was, of course, if it didn't tear us into pieces first.

'Paddy!' Marty screamed.

I turned my head to see the serpent continuing to chase the office chair as it bumped along the golf course. But that wasn't what caught my attention.

Beyond the snake I saw the glimmer of sunlight on iron golf clubs as a buggy came tearing down the fairway. Behind the wheel was Mr Ridgeman, his face a menacing twist and his eyes set on the serpent. Five other people clung to the side of the cart waving their clubs.

We needed to get it to the creek before it was too late.

I lifted my bottom off the seat and pushed as hard as I could. My legs felt like they were about to catch alight. My knuckles were white as I gripped the handlebars.

The creek was no more than thirty metres ahead.

I glanced back to see the serpent still thrashing towards Marty in the office chair. The golf buggy still tearing up the fairway behind the serpent.

I turned and saw a giant bunker right in front of me. A rise in the turf had hidden it from view until now. I squeezed the brakes as hard as I could, but fell into the pit of sand and came to a sudden stop. I looked up, hearing Marty's scream grow louder, and watched as the office chair flew off the rise and over the top of the bunker. In mid-air, the rope pulled tight.

I watched in horror as Marty shot out from his chair at the speed of a bullet. He splashed into the creek and out of sight. A moment later, the serpent slithered past me and into the water.

'Marty!' I ran as fast as I could towards the bank.

I could hear the screeching brakes of the buggy behind me. The golfers' faces were now painted with fear.

'HELP!' I pleaded, pointing towards the water. 'My friend, Marty. Help!' I couldn't get the words out.

I was about to dive in after Marty but

a hand grabbed my shoulder. It was Mr
Ridgeman.

'Stop!' he yelled, his eyes on the creek. 'It's
too dangerous.'

I halted and looked out at the water. It
was calm. Silent. There was no sign of Marty.
No sign of the serpent. Not a ripple on the
surface. Marty had disappeared. My friend
was gone.

'Marty!' I screamed.

I turned towards Mr Ridgeman, who was
looking at his fellow golfers in sadness. Then
one of the men looked up, his face filled with
shock as he pointed. One by one they all
followed his gaze.

I turned around. I couldn't believe what I
was seeing. Rising high out of the water was
the serpent. Its shimmering steel-blue body
standing strong. Its bright yellow eyes on
mine. Its mouth open wide.

And inside its mouth lay Marty. His eyes
closed. His body limp.

The serpent moved towards the creek edge.

Mr Ridgeman and his golfers took a step backwards. I stood my ground and watched as the serpent slowly lowered Marty to the shore.

Marty didn't move. His eyes didn't open.

I watched in shock as the serpent lifted its head above Marty's. With a flick of its tongue, it licked his face from chin to forehead, leaving a trail of fluorescent green slime.

Almost instantly, Marty started to move. His eyes opened. Marty stared into the serpent's eyes, but he wasn't scared. He wasn't shocked. He smiled.

The rest of us watched as the serpent smiled back, before turning and submerging itself in the creek without leaving a single ripple.

We looked out at the water in awe for what felt like minutes before Marty stood up.

'Hey, Mr Ridgeman.' Marty gestured at the creek. 'You owe my dad a new office chair.'

'**A-one, a-two,** a-one, two, three, go!'

Marty smashed the skins of the drums and hit the cymbals like a monkey on a sugar high. I strummed the strings so hard and fast my guitar sounded like Dad's whipper snipper. We were out of tune. We were out of time. But we didn't care. We were finally a band playing our first show at Top Hill Golf Club in front of twenty elderly patrons who had already flicked their hearing aids off. I guess they couldn't handle the rocking sounds of The Serpent Riders.

The Letterbox

'**It's too** early!' I mumbled from underneath my pillow.

'**Too early?**' I could hear Dad pulling open my curtains. 'Well, the birds are chirping and that's good enough for me!'

But I couldn't hear any birds. All I could hear was Mum's wind chimes smashing against each other. Which meant one thing: the winter winds had kicked in. It was going to be freezing outside.

Dad pulled the pillow away from my head. 'C'mon, get up.'

The floorboards felt like

under my toes

'Argh!' I pulled myself out of bed and squinted at my watch: 5.11 a.m. The floorboards felt like ice under my toes.

I looked enviously at Troy, who continued to sleep with his pinky finger jammed into his nostril.

Dad gave me one of his signature nudges as I rubbed my arms to warm them up.

'The papers don't deliver themselves. Go on.'

I struggled to pedal and brake down Hellman's Hill, the steepest hill in Top Hill. My face and fingers were numb as the gale-force winds pounded them. My nose rhythmically sniffled in time with the squeeze of the brakes. I had to work hard to keep my balance and not go over the handlebars as the back wheel struggled to stick to the steep slope.

It's not unusual for Top Hill to be windy. It's what you get when you live on one of the tallest hills in Australia. But cold weather is not something we're used to. And when you combine the two, it's what our local weather reporter calls an 'unpredictable weather event'.

THE *STEEPEST* HILL IN *Top Hill!*

windy

TOP HILL

I'd call it an 'unfair weather event'. As in, it was unfair that in my first few weeks as a paperboy I was forced to be out in it at five o'clock in the morning. Do people even read newspapers anymore?

Every time I started to gain momentum on the bike, I had to force myself to a stop and slip another newspaper into a letterbox. The next letterbox was one of the worst. It has a star-shaped tube that is designed to fit a newspaper for an ant. I have yet to squeeze a newspaper in there successfully without tearing the first few pages.

Most houses on my paper run look the same. Same red brick.

Star-shaped
TUBE

I have yet to squeeze
a newspaper in successfully
without tearing the first few pages.

Same concrete driveway. Same red
bottlebrush tree in the small front
yard. The only thing that changes
from house to house is the
letterbox. And there are many types
of letterboxes out there. I already
have a name for them all.

BASIC
BOX

The Basic Box is a small
box on a thin pole. The more
advanced model has the
newspaper tube on the side.
Nothing fancy, hence the name.

BASIC
BOX
(advanced)

newspaper
tube on
the side

Then you have the Goliath Box.
Either cement or brick, it stands
almost a metre high with a
neat built-in box and tube.
These are my favourite as the
tube is usually big enough to fit
two papers. Sometimes I'm able
to slip the paper into the tube
without stopping.
Speedy service.

GOLIATH
BOX

aRtSy FaRtSy

wooden peg

half a cog

corrugated iron

nut

fork

spoon

Then you have the Artsy Fartsy Boxes. These are usually homemade. Some are models of the actual house. Or magical frozen chains holding an odd-shaped box. Or a mess of scrap metal formed in the shape of an animal. Most of these look terrible. And they rarely have a tube installed.

I have a choice of either attempting to squeeze the thick Saturday paper into the thin mail slot or chucking it on the ground. The ground wins, hands down.

I shouldn't really complain. We don't even have a letterbox. Dad just stapled the number of our house to the tree out the front and drew an arrow with black marker to the fork of the lowest branch. But now that the tree has grown, no one can reach the lowest branch. So Dad put out an old broken crate beside it.

Different shapes, colours, sizes. Some numbered. Some unnumbered. Some numbers

44

upside down. Every letterbox gives a little insight into its owners.

Pedal, pedal, brake. I continued to stop and start down the hill. My face was completely numb. My fingers were burning. I was almost at the bottom of the hill.

The best part about this paper route was the fact that all the houses are on one side of the road. The opposite side of the road is bushland. It makes it easier to walk my bike back up to the top of Hellman's Hill. But Dad reckons it won't be long until it all becomes new houses.

For now, I enjoyed being able to quickly make my way back to the top. But it didn't come quick enough after having to deliver the last paper to **number 71**.

Everyone feared number 71. Rumour had it that the last two paper deliverers quit the route because of number 71. Number 71 was at the very bottom of the hill, tucked away in the bushland on the other side of the road.

The house was small, with cracked fibro walls. Remnants of ancient grey paint flaked off the exterior. Instead of blinds, the windows were roughly painted black, with scratch marks revealing a dim orange glow pulsing inside. But it wasn't the house that made my spine tingle. It was the letterbox.

The letterbox was once solid timber. That was about a hundred years ago. With the wood rotten and eaten away by various critters, it had been patched up with pieces of scrap metal. These too had been eaten away over time by rust, leaving jagged tooth-like pieces shaped in an angry snarl, warning anyone who came too close of impending danger. I had named it the **Beast Box**.

There wasn't a tube on the box. There wasn't a pole either. No, the worst thing about the Beast Box wasn't the way it looked. It was the fact that it was attached to the front door.

THE BEAST

attached to the FRONT DOOR!

Finally, I had reached the bottom of the hill.
The wind was blowing stronger than ever.
I felt as if I was going to be blown over like
piece of paper, or even worse, sucked into the
bushland.

Forcing my way across the road, I glanced at number 71. The trees that surrounded it danced angrily, almost warning me to stay away. The chain link fence thrashed against the rusty posts, sending up an ear-piercing shrill. The loosely fixed 'DO NOT LEAVE PAPER ON THE GROUND' sign slammed against the fence, sternly ordering me to make my way to the Beast Box.

The driveway, covered in large, jagged stones, was too much for my bike. I'd tried it once before, resulting in a puncture of both my tyres. I rested my bike against the chain link fence, grabbed the last paper from my bag and began the treacherous journey down the rugged driveway.

Every step I took forced the giant rocks under my feet to clap together. Loud enough to pierce the wind and signal to whoever was inside that someone was approaching. There was no way of tiptoeing. Each step I took clicked and clacked, creating tightness in my chest.

A giant wind gust pushed me
off balance, making my feet dance
over the rocks. As they shifted under
me, I lost my balance and fell
hard to the ground.
I wanted to yell
out in pain, but I
knew that would alert
whoever lurked
inside the house.

CLACK
CLACK

I took a few deep breaths
and struggled back to my feet. I checked my
arms and legs. Both were grazed. My left
hand had a deep cut from catching the edge
of a sharp rock, preventing my face from
damage. But there was no time to worry
about it now.

I carefully moved across the rocks and
picked up the newspaper before locking eyes
with the Beast Box. This was it, I thought.
I was going to make a dash for it. I would
leave the newspaper on top of the Beast Box,
then turn and sprint back to my bike. I would

49

push it up the hill faster than a swooping magpie. And after today, I too would quit this paper route. I was sick of risking my life just to deliver a measly newspaper.

I took a giant sniff before running as fast as my aching legs could take me along the shifting rocks. My ankles twisted on the uneven surface. I skidded to a stop as I reached the front door. I tossed the paper on top of the letterbox but it fell. I quickly moved forward and picked it up.

That's when I heard the lock on the door click. I was just in time to see the doorhandle turn as I swiftly placed the newspaper on top of the Beast Box. My heart stopped. But my legs didn't. I turned and ran.

That was when my toes caught the sharp edge of a rock and I fell face down with a crash. I didn't have time to absorb the pain. I jumped up and continued to run gingerly down the driveway.

My entire body hurt. I tried to sprint but my legs were jelly. The wind wasn't helping either. It was pushing me towards the house, almost as if the Beast Box was sucking me towards it.

I struggled on, my ankles twisting and straining against the uneven terrain. At no time did I look back. For all I knew, there was no one behind me. I didn't care to find out. I continued to stagger along until finally I made it to my bike.

I grabbed the handlebars and tried to push my bike towards the road – but it wouldn't budge. I pushed harder and harder. Nothing.

I looked down to see the pedal tangled up in the rusty chain link fence. The wind pounded the fence against my bike, making it almost impossible to find where the pedal was stuck.

I quickly sat down and threw my feet against the fence in an attempt to force the pedal free. But it was stuck fast. I gritted my teeth and pulled harder and harder.

Suddenly the bike separated itself from the fence and pinned me down. I pushed it off me and saw that the pedal had been ripped off and was lying on the other side of the fence. I reached through a metal loop to grab it.

That's when a hand grabbed my wrist.

I froze in fear as a shadow grew over me. I forced myself to look up along the gripping arm to see a small old man with a head of frizzy hair. His giant wire-framed glasses sat tightly against his bony cheeks. The

A small OLD MAN with a head of frizzy hair

old man loosened his grip and picked up the broken pedal before looking at me with his cold, grey eyes.

I couldn't help myself. I **SCREAMED** at the top of my lungs. It was louder than the wind against the chain link fence. It drowned out the heavy rustling of the swaying trees.

I stood up and sprinted all the way up the hill. Dogs were barking. Car alarms began to ring. I didn't care. I just wanted to be as far away from number 71 as possible.

I ran out of breath just outside my house. Panting, I scurried inside, locked the door and ran to my room, throwing my head back under my pillow. As my heart raced at a million miles per hour I promised myself that I would never return to the bottom of the hill as long as I lived.

I didn't leave my room on Sunday, even though Troy kept coming in to annoy me every five minutes. On Monday, I felt embarrassed. Tuesday, disappointed. By Wednesday, I was angry. Angry that I had left my prized possession at the bottom of the hill to rust away like everything else at number 71. By Friday afternoon I had built up enough courage to return.

I waited until Saturday came around. Paper day. This time, I got out of bed before sunrise. I left the newspapers on the front doorstep and stormed down the hill.

By the time I had reached the bottom the sun had peeked over the horizon. I decided that I was going to approach the old man and demand the return of my bike. I could see the chain link fence. I could see the jagged path. I could see the house. And that's when I saw my bike against the Beast Box. Well, I thought it was my bike. There was something odd about it.

I took a deep breath and walked up the driveway. This time I strode more confidently over the rugged rocks, trying to stay composed. I was going to quickly take my bike and return home.

As I got closer, I noticed the pedal had been reattached. But in addition, something had been attached to the bike's frame. It was a giant circle with many small tubes on the outside. Similar to the tubes attached to letterboxes.

Attached to the giant circle, a thick pipe ran to a box behind the seat. On the box were printed the words **'LOAD PAPERS HERE'**.

A thin blue wire ran from the box along the frame and up the handlebars. Attached to the handlebars was a smaller box with a keyhole and a red button with a word inked on top: **'SHOOT'**.

I couldn't believe what I was seeing. The old man had modified my bike. It looked incredible!

From the corner of my eye, I saw something glimmer in the rising sun. I turned to see a key dangling from the rusty snarl on the Beast Box. I reached over and carefully removed the key from the sharp steel. Hesitantly, I put it in the keyhole on my handlebars and turned.

The old man had MODIFIED my bike!

Immediately, the giant circle began to rapidly spin. I quickly turned it off. I didn't want to wake the old man.

I looked up at the house. That's when I noticed a smiling face had been scratched into the black paint on the window. An orange light glowed from inside the house, making the smiling face seem warm. Welcoming.

I smiled back at the window before carrying my bike along the rocks and on to the road. As I stood beside my bike, I looked back at the house. It looked different now. The chain link fence sat still against its posts. The trees

had been SCRATCHED into the black paint on the window.

surrounding the house swayed gently in the breeze. Number 71 looked peaceful.

Still smiling, I walked my bike up the hill.

It took some time to get used to, but my modified bike became a sensation. Once the box was loaded with papers, they would push through the pipe and into the tubes around the giant circle. When the button on the handlebars was pressed, the tubes would shoot a paper into each letterbox. I could shoot papers from fifty metres away without missing a target. And the best part was, I never had to stop pedalling.

After a short time, the owner of the newspaper, Mrs Chambers, gave me more and more delivery routes. People began to gather out the front of their houses to get a glimpse of the bike in action. Some people even moved their letterboxes to different places to test my aim. Still, I never missed.

People clapped and cheered every Saturday as I sailed through their street. Other kids on bikes would follow me for kilometres. I had become a celebrity.

The Basic, Goliath, Artsy Fartsy all felt the full force of the paper-shooter. Even the star-shaped tubes became easy targets. I used the device to deliver every paper.

All except one.

At the bottom of the hill at number 71, I hand-deliver the newspaper to the Beast Box. I haven't seen the old man since that day, but I know he is watching. Watching his magical invention do wonders from the scratches on his black painted windows.

The Perfect Point

'Samantha Foster, B.'

Samantha smiled at Tina Vu, both acknowledging their rewarding results.

'Ifraan Ghazali, B.'

Ifraan high-fived Cameron Bird. Both were happy with their marks.

I put my head on my desk. I didn't want to see them all looking at me. I could only hope she wouldn't read it out.

'Paddy Thompson, E.'

There wcrc gasps and mumbles around the room. I don't know why. It wasn't like it

came as a shock. Everyone knows I'm a bad
writer. Everyone knows I can't string two
sentences together. It's not like I can't read.
Or do maths. Or even talk properly. I just
can't write well. I mean, my handwriting is
all right. But what use is neat handwriting
when the words I write down don't make
sense? And it doesn't help that Mrs Brown
is the most boring teacher I've ever had.
I don't think I've lasted a single writing
lesson without my eyelids drooping.

'**Quiet please!**' Mrs Brown demanded.

The bell for lunch rang. Everyone stood up and started leaving the room. I avoided their stares by pretending to find something in my tidy tray. I was embarrassed. Ashamed.

I started putting my pencil case in my desk when Mrs Brown approached.

'That's two Es for writing this term, Paddy.' Mrs Brown placed my paper on my desk. It was a Picasso of red pen with a giant E circled a dozen times on the top corner of the page, just to rub it in.

'I know, Mrs Brown,' I replied grimly.

'Well, Mr Thompson, you'll need at least a C on your next assessment to pass Literacy.' Mrs Brown's beady eyes burned into mine.

'Yes, Mrs Brown,' I replied, my tone still flat.

'And you know what happens if you don't pass Literacy, don't you, Mr Thompson?'

'Yes, Mrs Brown; I have to repeat grade five.'

Mrs Brown continued to stare at me with

her beady eyes. I was too scared to blink. Too afraid to breathe. It felt like an eternity.

She finally stood up and started walking back to her desk.

'Go to lunch now, Paddy.'

'Yes, Mrs Brown.'

I stood up and left the classroom as quickly as I could.

A week passed and any motivation I'd felt about writing something passable had gone out the window. I hadn't written a thing. I'd come up with every possible excuse to avoid doing the task. But now, it was due tomorrow.

I sat on my bed and looked at the assessment task Mrs Brown had given us. A two-page argumentative essay on why wood is better than metal. Like I said before, Mrs Brown is the most boring teacher in the universe.

I felt like Mrs Brown had also sprinkled a little bit of her drowsy-dust on the paper, as I felt my body begging to crawl under the covers and never come out.

Mum stopped at my bedroom door. She must have seen the worry on my face.

'You feeling crook, mate?'

'I wish,' I said as I sat back up. 'Then I wouldn't have to write this stupid assignment.'

Mum walked in and sat on the end of the bed.

'You know, if you're really that stuck for ideas, you could always go and ask Paul next door.'

My eyes widened. Mum was right. Why hadn't I thought of it sooner? Paul Paynter was going to save me.

I jumped out of bed, grabbed the assignment off my desk and hurried out of my room.

'Thanks, Mum,' I called from the hallway. 'I'm going next door.'

According to Mum, our neighbour, Paul Paynter, was once a world-renowned journalist. Back in the 1970s, he used to travel the world writing stories about anything and everything. He got to interview world leaders and famous artists and attend significant events, which resulted in Paul winning heaps of awards. Other journalists even started writing about him!

But then, Mum told me, without any warning, he stopped writing. He left the high life and disappeared into the normal world.

Paul was a quiet, friendly neighbour. He rarely left his house unless it was to get groceries or collect the newspapers from his driveway. I have never seen someone buy so many newspapers. Each day, a pile as high as his letterbox would be delivered. Papers from all around the world. England, Japan, Brazil, Iceland. When I delivered his paper on Saturdays, he would always smile and wave as he carried the other twenty from his driveway. Unlike our 'new' neighbours on the other side of the house, Paul had lived next to us for as long as I could remember.

But now, I needed more than a friendly smile. I needed a neighbourly favour.

I knocked on the door and took a step back. I could hear the muffled sound of a television inside. Thinking that he may not have heard me, I stepped forward to knock again, a little louder. The door immediately swung open.

'Hello?' Paul's eyes adjusted to the sunlight. He was dressed in an old pair of tracksuit pants and a T-shirt that read 'Happy Easter'. It was December.

'Uh, hello, Mr Paynter,' I stumbled. 'It's me, Paddy from next door.'

Paul pulled his glasses down from his head. He instantly recognised who I was and opened the screen door.

'Well, good morning, Paddy. It is still morning, right?'

'It's um, about three-thirty,' I politely corrected.

'Ah, it's morning somewhere around the world.' He chuckled. 'Come on in.'

I stepped into the house. It was now me who had to adjust my eyes. It was dark. All the blinds were closed. Other than a few old dusty lamps, all the lights were off. Paul's room was lit up by not one, not two, but five giant television sets. Each TV played a different news station with headlines in all different languages.

'So, how can I help you, Paddy?' Paul asked as we dodged the thousands upon thousands of newspapers stacked on the floor.

'I, um, have an assignment due tomorrow...'

'Is it on politics? Hollywood movies? Alien invasions?'

'Actually, it's on wood.'

Paul stopped and turned back with a confused expression.

'Wood?'

'And metal,' I stated.

'I see,' he replied matter-of-factly. 'Well, that sounds a little boring.'

I chuckled. It was true. He was right.

'My biggest problem is I don't know how I

should write it,' I continued. 'And Mum said you're a pretty good writer, and—'

'So you need help writing it, then?' Paul interrupted.

'**Could you?**' I asked.

Paul rubbed his grey beard before clicking his fingers.

'Hang on two ticks. Let me grab a few things.'

On that note, Paul mazed his way around the newspapers and disappeared into another room.

I stood there looking around at the house. At all the old newspapers covered in dust. All the television screens sharing pictures from around the world in languages I had never seen before.

And that's when I saw the glass cabinet. The light from the televisions flickered on rows of shiny objects. I walked over to see it up close. I couldn't believe what I was seeing. Trophies and medals. Old photos of Paul with celebrities dressed in fancy clothes. In a frame was the front page of a magazine

with Paul's face in the middle. The caption 'Greatest Writer of All Time?' was underneath. Mum was right; Paul was famous!

But among all his prized possessions, on a shelf of its own, sat a glass box. And inside the glass box sat a lead pencil. A lead pencil unlike any pencil I had ever seen. Its body was bright green. A green so bright it appeared to glow. Spiralling around the illuminating pencil was a pink stripe. My eyes followed the line all the way to the tip of the pencil. To the sharpest lead I had ever seen. The perfect point.

I could hear Paul sifting through papers in the other room. I couldn't help myself. I had to hold the pencil.

I carefully reached into the cabinet and opened the glass box. I lifted the pencil off its perch. It was heavier than I expected. I studied it in awe. It was the most beautiful pencil I had ever seen. Its pink stripe hypnotised me. Its green glow shone warmly into my unblinking eyes.

THE SHARPEST
LEAD I HAD EVER SEEN

I was so captivated by the pencil that I didn't see the stack of newspapers behind me. I bumped into them, overbalanced, and slipped. Papers flew into the air. So did my legs. I felt like I floated in mid-air before finally hitting the floor hard. My bottom hurt, but not as much as the searing pain in my right hand.

'Everything all right out there?' Paul called.

I quickly stood up and shook my hand.

'Yeah, I'm fine,' I lied. 'Just some newspapers fell over.'

'Ah, that's okay,' Paul replied, continuing to rifle through his drawers. 'Happens all the time.'

I looked frantically for the pencil. Thanks to the glow of the televisions, the pink stripe of the pencil reflected behind a sheet of newspaper. I snatched it off the ground and quietly sat it back inside the glass box. I took a step back from the cupboard. And that's when I saw something that made my heart skip a beat. The tip of the lead pencil was missing. It had been snapped off.

I knew instantly what had happened. I knew exactly where the tip of the pencil had gone. I looked down at my throbbing right hand. Deep in the palm between my pinky and ring finger was a dot. A dot that flashed green and pink under my skin.

The TIP of the lead was MISSING

'Rightio.'

Paul wove his way back into the living room. I quickly threw my hand behind my back.

'This is an old journal made from recycled wood and these two pens are aluminium. Let's get started.'

'I'm sorry, Mr Paynter, but I just heard Dad calling for me,' I lied.

'Oh, I didn't hear a thing,' Paul said. 'But then again, these ears don't work like they used to.'

'Thanks anyway, Mr Paynter.'

I turned and hastily made for the door. I needed to escape before he found out.

'**Hey!**' Paul called.

I froze in fear. He knew. I was in a world of trouble.

'Let me know how you go.'

'Thanks,' I said, then bolted back to my house.

I ran my hand under the tap for almost an hour. Eventually, the throbbing stopped. I tried using tweezers to pull the glowing lead from my hand like a splinter. But it was no use. It was lodged too deep.

I looked at the clock. It was already past five and I hadn't even started my assessment. I was doomed.

I couldn't eat dinner. My stomach was in a

mass of knots. The combination of knowing
I was about to fail Literacy and the fact that I
had ruined my neighbour's prized possession
made me feel ill.

I went up to my room and sat at my desk.
I opened my exercise book and stared at the
blank page. I couldn't find the energy to pick
up my pen. I dropped my head on the book
and gave up.

I woke to the sound of the newspaper
delivery truck taking off after dropping a
hundred papers on Paul Paynter's driveway.
I was still at my desk. My back ached from
sleeping in my hard desk chair. But that pain
was forgotten the moment I remembered what
day it was. Assessment day. The day I was
going to fail Literacy. The day I say goodbye
to going to grade six.

I looked down at the closed exercise book.
I decided the only thing I could do was
write a quick apology to Mrs Brown for not

finishing my assignment. Maybe she would be understanding. Maybe she would let me off with a warning. Deep down I knew that was impossible.

I opened my book and gasped.

The paper was no longer blank. There was page after page of handwriting. *My* handwriting. I knew it was my handwriting because of the particular way I write my Zs and Fs. And the way I dot my Is a little to the right. I quickly read a few lines to find it was the essay I needed. It was all there. All mine.

But how?

I was startled by a knock on my door.

'Time to get up, Paddy,' Mum called.

'I'm awake,' I replied, still staring in disbelief at the essay.

I didn't have time to think about how it got there. I had to go – to hopefully pass my Literacy class.

I was about to find out my future. I had handed in my assessment without reading it. And ever since, Mrs Brown had been staring at me with her beady black eyes. I could see her reading it. I could see her face twitching. Her head shaking. Her long wiry fingers tapping the table. And then I saw her red pen making circle after circle.

Mrs Brown stood from her desk.

'Class, your writing assessments have been marked and I have your results.'

Everyone sat up tall in their seats. Everyone except for me. I just wanted to get this over with.

'But before I begin, I must acknowledge one student who has stood out from the rest. One student who has written an assessment so good, it could be published in *Australian Scientific* magazine.'

The class started mumbling to one another. Students started to shrug their shoulders. Some pointed at Jessica Goldwin. She was by far the best writer in our class. By the smile on her face, even Jessica thought Mrs Brown was referring to her.

'This piece of writing is so good, it could change the way we think about the relationship between wood and metal.'

The mumbling continued to grow. Mrs Brown started walking towards me.

'This piece of writing is so good,' she continued as she approached my desk, 'that it is too good to be true.'

Mrs Brown slammed the paper on my desk.

'And for that reason, Mr Thompson, you have failed Literacy.'

Everyone gasped. Then the room was silent. I looked down at my paper. Circled at least a dozen times in red pen was the word **'CHEATER'.**

Mr Gill, the school principal, sat at his desk reading through my assessment. Every now and then he looked up at me with a confused expression. Mrs Brown sat beside me with her

arms crossed, her eyes darting between my paper and me.

I tried not to sink into my chair. I didn't want Mr Gill to think I had copied my assignment. I had written it. I don't know how, but it was definitely my handwriting. There was no way anyone else in my house could have written it. I've seen my parents' shopping lists. There must not have been spelling back when they went to school.

Mr Gill lifted his head from the paper and

looked me in the eye. The deep wrinkles on his forehead formed a stern arrow.

'So, Mr Thompson, where exactly did you copy this from?'

I could feel Mrs Brown's beady eyes burning into the side of my head.

'I didn't copy it.' I could hear the desperation in my voice. 'I swear, Mr Gill, this is my work.'

Mr Gill looked over at Mrs Brown. The wrinkles on his head didn't move.

'According to your past results, Mr Thompson...' He stood up from his desk with the paper in his hand. 'This seems almost impossible.'

Mr Gill tossed my assignment on his desk. I didn't know what to say. He was right. It was impossible. I couldn't explain how the writing got there. How ten pages of beautifully crafted work appeared overnight.

I looked up at Mr Gill.

'I can prove it,' I stated.

Mr Gill and Mrs Brown looked at each other in surprise.

'I can prove that my writing is amazing.'

Mr Gill scratched his bald head.

'And how do you intend to prove this?' he asked.

Mrs Brown started tapping her foot on the floor. Mr Gill put his hands in his pockets.

'Give me a topic,' I answered. 'Anything at all. I'll prove to you both that I am a fantastic writer.'

Mr Gill looked over at Mrs Brown, then back at me.

'Anything?' he asked.

'Anything,' I repeated.

With her arms still crossed, Mrs Brown stood up and walked over to Mr Gill. Smirks appeared on their faces as they looked at each other.

'All right, Mr Thompson,' said Mrs Brown, the smirk still spread across her face, 'I want you to write about a flying cane toad.'

'And the flying cane toad has a sausage dressed as a ballerina for a friend,' Mr Gill added.

SMIRKS appeared on their FACES!

'And the cane toad is allergic to insects.'

'And the sausage has a purple moustache.'

'And together, they save the day,' Mrs Brown finished.

I was stunned. I mean, this was the most ridiculous thing I had ever heard. How did they expect me to write about that?

'And you can do it right here,' Mr Gill insisted. 'In my office after lunch.'

I was done. Dead meat. But I couldn't help myself.

'Sounds perfect.'
★ ★ ✦

I sat at a small table in the corner of the office while Mr Gill sorted through piles of papers on his desk. I kept my pencil busy to avoid gaining his attention. If he looked closely, he would see that I was writing the words 'flying cane toad' over and over.

The only good thing about being in Mr Gill's office was the air conditioning. It was set at the lowest temperature possible – just low enough to stop the nervous beads of sweat from dripping down my face.

'How are you going, Mr Thompson?' Mr Gill asked, making me sit up straight in my chair.

'It's sounding great,' I lied.

That's when he stood up.

'Really?' he asked. 'I'd love to see it.'

Mr Gill started walking around his desk. This was it. The moment I was found out. The moment that I, Paddy Thompson, become known as the biggest cheater of all time.

But just as Mr Gill drew closer to my table, his office door swung open, making a loud bang as it hit the wall. Mr Gill and I turned our heads like a shot. Mrs Beaman, the school administrator, stood in the doorway with her hands on her hips, breathing heavily. I felt the heat of the summer day invade the room.

'Mr Gill, we have a Code Two,' she gasped between heavy breaths.

Mr Gill started towards the door.

'Code Two?' he asked.

'Yes, Jaden is on the roof again!'

Mr Gill hurried out the door. Mrs Beaman followed, closing it behind her. I was all alone in the principal's office.

I didn't know what to do. I sat and looked at my paper. It was a mess. I scrunched it into a ball and tossed it in the bin.

I picked up my pencil and stared at the blank piece of paper in front of me. At all the empty space between the blue lines. As empty as the thoughts in my brain. I had nothing. I dropped the pencil onto the desk and put my head in my hands.

I decided to give up. When Mr Gill returned I would tell him I didn't write my assignment. I would lie and tell him I found it on the internet.

I could feel the cool breeze of the air conditioning on the back of my neck. There are no air conditioners in the classrooms. We don't even have one at home. The feeling of the cold air hitting my skin made me relax in my chair. It made my brain stop worrying about my problems. It made my eyes heavy. And before I knew it, I fell asleep.

★ ★ ★

'I didn't do nuffin!'

I was startled awake by the loud voice of another student. I looked across to see Jaden Jackson enter the office. His school shirt was covered in dirt and he wasn't wearing any shoes.

Behind Jaden was Mr Gill. His shirt was saturated and also covered in dirt. Beads of sweat were dancing down his forehead wrinkles.

85

Jaden threw himself on the floor in the corner of the room and leaned his head against the wall. Mr Gill walked over and stood under the air conditioner. He aimed his red, bald head at the vents.

'All right,' he said, and turned towards me. 'You finished?'

My eyes grew wide. I had completely forgotten why I was here. I had forgotten about being exposed as a 'cheater'.

I turned around to grab my paper and hand it to Mr Gill. But when I saw it, my heart stopped. I couldn't believe what I was looking at. Sitting on the table was the paper. But it wasn't empty. There was page after page of neat handwriting underneath my pencil. The high crossed Ts and the Is dotted to the right. My handwriting. My work. My story.

Mr Gill leaned over and grabbed the pages.

'Well, Mr Thompson, it seems you have been busy.'

All I could do was nod. It was more of a nod of disbelief than agreement.

Mr Gill sat at his desk and started reading my story. I sat in my chair twiddling the pencil. I was nervous. I had no idea what I had written. No idea whether it made any sense.

Every now and then I could see a twitch in Mr Gill's wrinkles. I could see his face turning pink like Jaden's sunburn. Eventually he stopped reading. He stood up from behind his desk.

This was it.

This was when I would fail grade five.

Mr Gill's face continued to grow red. His lips were pressed tightly together. His eyes started filling up with water. I could feel it. He was about to explode with anger.

But then he did something I never expected. Even Jaden jumped up in fright. Mr Gill burst out in a hysterical laugh. So loud it knocked the pencil out of my hand.

'Mr Thompson!' he cackled, holding the pages above his head. 'This is the funniest thing I have read in my entire life! Pure genius!'

That's when I smiled. I knew I was bound for grade six.

★ ★ ★

I walk onto the red carpet. Cameras begin to click and flash in my direction. 'Paddy, can I get a selfie?' says one of my fans, who has come out to celebrate the release of my twentieth bestselling book, *The Perfect Point*. I lean in and give a smile.

I look around at the thousands of people all holding a copy of my latest novel, waving them in the air as a desperate plea to get me to sign them. Among the crazy parade of people stands someone familiar.

It's Paul Paynter. He gives me a wink. I wink back. We know how this writing works. How to use the pencil's magic. Our secret is safe.

I continue to walk down the red carpet. Standing at the end is a reporter holding a microphone.

'Paddy, Paddy!' the reporter calls for me. She too has stars in her eyes. 'You must tell us, what is the secret to your success?'

I look back to where Paul Paynter was standing. He has disappeared.

'The secret,' I begin, 'is to have a good night's sleep.'

The Nudge

It was
SCORCHING

Some people have pools. Others live near the beach or a river. We had a lousy hose and sprinkler. And on days like this, they just didn't do the job. To say it was hot was like saying Godzilla is tall. It was scorching.

Droplets of my sweat hit the concrete slab and sizzled. There wasn't a single patch of shade, not even under the verandah.

We live on one of the tallest hills in all of Australia, so you'd think there'd be some breeze, but it was as still as a rotting cane toad.

And of course, Mum decided today would be the best day to **BUG-BOMB** the house.

Mum sometimes does things without thinking them through. For example, she made Dad move all the lounge room furniture around last month, before realising there weren't any power points near the television. So for a week, we had an extension lead running right through the middle of the room. It was back to its original layout the following weekend.

So it was no big surprise when Mum decided to send us all outside in the blistering summer heat while the cool indoors was filled with poisonous gas.

Troy and I sat cross-legged on the lawn beside the sprinkler, waiting for it to rotate

to our faces. We were disappointed when the water that hit our heads was hot. Not warm. Hot.

Nina decided to make the most of the sun and squeezed an entire lemon onto her head to bleach her hair and make her look like a beach person. I'm pretty sure her almost see-through skin was enough to show she wasn't a beach person. But there she sat, on a towel on the lawn, smelling like a citrus tree.

Mum had set up a giant umbrella for her and Bella to sit under. Bella sat naked in her shell pool with all her bath toys. Mandy, our Maltese dog, had her head in the pool slurping up the water. Mum sat beside Bella reading one of her gossip magazines and drinking an iced coffee that she had just poured from her thermal mug.

Troy and I jumped to our feet as Dad pulled into the driveway. He'd texted to say he was bringing home something exciting. I hoped it was an outdoor air conditioner or a giant ice cube to lie on. But it wasn't. Dad opened the boot of the car and pulled out a giant roll of black plastic.

'What are we going to do with that?' I asked, annoyed.

Dad didn't say anything. He shuffled past me and dropped the roll onto the front lawn.

He wiped his forehead with his shirt before giving me one of his 'whatcha-reckon?' nudges.

Troy dropped his shoulders and returned to the sprinkler.

Before I could say anything, Dad found the end of the roll, pulled two tent pegs from his back pocket and pushed them through the black plastic into the ground. He checked that it was secure, then pushed the rest of the roll down the hill. I watched as it unfurled over every driveway in our street. It continued to roll until I could no longer see it.

Dad returned to the boot and came back with a bottle of fluorescent green liquid. I read the label on the bottle.

Kevin's Kwiklid: The Kwikest Liquid in the Southern Hemisphere.

KEVIN'S KWIKLID

THE KWIKEST LIQUID IN THE SOUTHERN HEMISPHERE

WARNING: USE ONLY **1** CAPFUL AT A TIME. EXCESSIVE KWIKLID CAN BE A REAL KILLER

Below that was a warning label with big bold lettering.

Dad opened the cap and poured the entire bottle onto the plastic.

'Well, go on then,' he said, again with his signature nudge.

'What, down there?' I responded, pointing down the steep face of Hellman's Hill.

'Look.' He walked over to the pool, picked up Mandy the dog, and brought her back. He put her on the plastic. She took off at the speed of light without blinking an eyelid. 'She loves it!'

SHE LOVES IT!

Dad was **crazy** if he thought I was going to follow Mandy down.

I turned to walk away and trod on a bindy. I yelped and began hopping on the spot. It was the perfect opportunity for Dad to give me one more nudge, and before I knew it my bum hit the black plastic and I was travelling faster than an air force jet down Hellman's Hill.

I could feel my cheeks pressing hard against my teeth. I wanted to close my eyes but the sheer speed of my descent wouldn't allow my eyelids to shut. Everything around me was a blur. My feet flicked up droplets of Kevin's Kwiklid into my eyes, up my nostrils and down my throat. It tasted horrible!

I slid past Marty's house and Debbie's house and Trent's house. Then past number 71 at the bottom of the hill, before entering the laneway at the end of the street. I wasn't slowing down. In fact, I was certain I was gaining speed.

I tried to look ahead to see how much further this **nightmare** slide had to go.

Through my blurry vision I could just make
out where it ended.

Unfortunately, it ended right at the summit
of the giant BMX jump Rossco's dad had built
him last year. It was so big only Rossco had
tried it and he broke both his arms. It looked
like I was going to be victim number two.

I tried to brace myself, but all I could
do was make fists and scrunch up my toes.
Rossco's jump was growing larger and larger,

ROSSCO'S GIANT BMX JUMP

like a tidal wave wrapped in black plastic.
I held my breath and waited for the impact.

I hit the jump at such speed that my body
was rocketed into the sky. I was ascending at
the velocity of a ballistic missile. I felt the
hairs on my head catch
alight. Even my
eyebrows were
smoking!

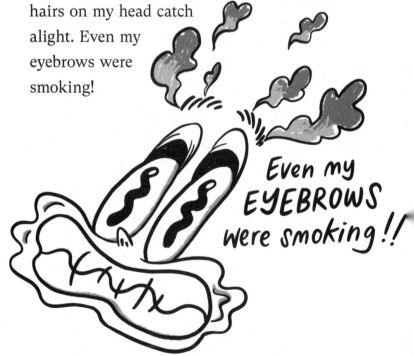

Even my
EYEBROWS
were smoking!!

I still couldn't move my arms or legs. Or close my eyelids.

The sky around me was growing darker. The air that I struggled to breathe was getting thinner and thinner. I was higher than any plane had ever been.

Gradually, I felt my cheeks loosen away from my teeth. I could move my arms and legs. My eyelids were beginning to flutter. I was slowing down.

I should have felt relief, but at thirty thousand metres in the sky I remembered something Mrs Brown once said to me.

'What goes up must come down.'

I shouldn't have, but I looked down. Big mistake. I could see the entire east coast of Australia. Although it was the most beautiful sight my twelve-year-old eyes had ever seen, I was overcome with fear as I felt myself start to fall.

I picked up speed as I dropped towards the ground. My arms and legs became stiff once more. My teeth met the inside of my cheeks and my eyelids locked themselves open. I was now travelling faster than I had in my ascent.

My eyebrows began to smoke again. My hair, or what was left of it, went back up in flames. This was it, I thought. I, Paddy Thompson, was about to hit the ground like a meteorite. I could only hope that I wouldn't feel the impact.

I forced my eyes to the right. I could see the Opera House in the distance. I forced them back to the left and thought I could see the Gateway Bridge in Brisbane. What was certain was that I was getting closer and closer to land.

Or maybe, just maybe, the sea.

I was beginning to notice less land and more ocean ahead of me. If I wasn't going to become a pancake on the land, I was definitely going to make the biggest splash known to humankind.

I fell and fell, and the ocean grew larger until it filled my field of vision. Again, I braced myself for impact. I made fists and scrunched up my toes.

Closer and closer. I held my breath.

I hit the water hard. But rather than sinking deep below the dark blue water, I bounced off like a pebble skipping across a lake. I was still moving at an incredible speed. It must be the Kevin's Kwiklid on my shorts!

My bottom continued to bounce off the surface of the water. Each skip felt like touching down on a cactus. I passed two cruise ships and watched as hundreds of sunburnt, cocktail-drinking adults gawked in disbelief as I bounced like a kangaroo in full flight across the top of the ocean. After around a hundred skips, my bottom went numb.

Finally I began to slow down. I could move my arms and legs again. My cheeks moved free from my teeth. My eyes were able to blink.

I looked ahead and saw a beautiful tropical island near the horizon. My backside continued to skim across the top of the water until I reached the rolling waves of the island's shoreline. Then my bottom hit a sand bar and I came to a dead stop.

The first thing I did was check my head. My suspicions were confirmed: it was as bald as my pop's. Fortunately, most of my eyebrows remained.

Then to my bottom. It was no use; it was still completely numb. One thing was for sure though, I definitely had a giant hole in my pants.

I gingerly stood up and staggered to shore. I noticed a number of people approaching me. All were wearing floral board shorts. A few of the bigger men had large tattoos. A couple of girls also wandered over.

All of them looked confused. They stared at me as if I'd fallen out of the sky. Well, to be fair, I had.

'Where am I?' I asked.

One of the tattooed men moved closer.

WELCOME TO SAMOA!

'*Talofa*. Welcome to Samoa.'

'**SAMOA!**' I shouted.

Everyone started laughing.

'Yes,' chuckled the man. 'My name is Fetuao, but you can call me Fetu.'

The laughing continued. Some people were laughing so hard they were on their hands and knees.

'And you are?' Fetu asked, a chuckle still in his voice.

That's when I saw it running towards me. A skinny, balding monster. Its tongue flapping from side to side. Saliva drooling from its lips. But as I looked closer, I realised it wasn't a monster at all. It was a hairless Maltese dog.

'Mandy!' I called out.

Everyone on the beach, including Fetu, laughed even louder.

I **won't** bore you with how Dad ended up paying for my flight back home. Let's just say he was a little less energetic with his signature nudge when I got off the plane.

Troy, on the other hand, couldn't stop patting my bald head. Bella just screamed when she saw me. Nina did the same when she saw a hairless Mandy.

All in all, I was the one smiling in the end. Even though I had a head like an egg, I got to escape the heat of Hellman's Hill with an overseas holiday. What more could I ask for?

A skinny, balding monster

Mannequins

It was the morning of the school disco.
Marty had been bugging me about it all week.

'Come on, Paddy!' he pleaded as we walked
to school. 'This is the biggest disco of the
year!'

'I dunno,' I answered. 'There'll be another
one.'

Marty stopped in his tracks, grabbed my
shoulders and stared straight into my eyes.

'But this is going to be the one that people
remember me for. I've been working on my
dance moves for weeks.'

I couldn't take it anymore. I could see how desperately he wanted to go.

'Whatever,' I finally conceded. 'I'll come.'

The truth was, I wanted to go. I wanted to go to all the discos. The bright, flashing lights. The loud, thumping music. The crazy dancing. So why was I being so hesitant about going? That's easy: my wardrobe.

If my wardrobe was a car it would have three wheels and leopard-spot paintwork, and would sound like a cat coughing up a fur ball. A total embarrassment. Marty's wasn't much better.

You see, our parents didn't have a lot of money. So when it came to clothing, it was straight down to CrazyMart for the best discounts. Although it was cheap, the fabric itched and hung off us like parachutes.

And when everyone turned up in their three-star sneakers and saw Marty and me in our fake two-star sneakers, I could feel them all laughing on the inside. Snickering at us. Especially Trent Rowe, the school bully.

Trent was always dressed in the most fashionable outfits from the posh shop, Kazaar Clothing. From shoes to shirts and jackets to jeans. He even dyed a blond streak through his dark hair just to prove to everyone how cool and rebellious he was. And he made it a goal of his to make anyone who dressed in no-name  clothing feel like dirt. Especially Marty and me.

'Really?' Marty shook my shoulders, bringing me back to reality. 'You'll really come to the disco?'

I smiled and gave a nod. You see, I really did want to go to this disco. Jemma Arrows was going. She is the most beautiful girl in school. And last week in class when Marty began nagging for me to go, Jemma had looked over at me and smiled. The kind of smile that said she was hoping I would say yes. It was then that I decided I was going to work up the courage to go to the disco and ask Jemma to dance with me. And I'd become one of the popular kids and live happily ever after.

The problem was, if someone as beautiful as Jemma Arrows was to dance with someone like me, I needed to find something **cool** to wear.

It was black with two red stripes running down the sleeves. It was made of real leather and had four shiny steel studs on the front pocket. It was the best jacket Marty and I had ever seen. It sat perfectly on the plastic mannequin inside Kazaar Clothing. The mannequin had a V-shaped scratch on its cheek, which made the jacket look extra tough. Cool and rebellious.

It was the same jacket we had seen Trent trying on two days ago. And by the look on his face, he'd known it was the coolest jacket in town. It was perfect.

'It's two hundred dollars,' Marty mumbled as he checked the price tag.

My heart sank. I didn't have two hundred dollars. Neither did Marty. We barely had enough money to buy new no-brand zip-up hoodies. And we needed them to hide whatever hideous shirts we had in our wardrobes. It was only a few hours until the start of the disco and we still had nothing to wear.

I turned to walk away, but Marty kept his eyes on the leather jacket.

'What if I just wore it for tonight?' he

COOL AND *REBELLIOUS*

said as he played with the shiny studs. 'And brought it back first thing tomorrow?'

I looked at Marty, puzzled.

'What do you mean?' I asked. 'Like, get a refund?'

'Not exactly,' he replied, his eyes still on the jacket. 'Just, you know, put it back where I found it?'

'You mean steal it?' I corrected.

Marty quickly covered my mouth.

'Are you crazy?' he whispered. 'You'll get us both in trouble.'

Marty removed his hand from my mouth just as my mum walked past the shopfront. Bella was sitting in the pram with bags hanging off the handles. Troy stood beside the pram making faces at her.

'All right.' Mum pulled a plain oversized shirt out of a bag. 'I got you this for the disco.' She tried to keep the pram in one spot, as Troy kept pulling it towards him.

'I better go.' I turned towards Marty. 'I'll see you at the disco.'

Marty fist-bumped me.

'It's going to be awesome.' He winked.

I warned, looking between Marty and the jacket. Marty gave me an unconvincing nod as I turned and headed out of the shop.

★ ★ ★

Flashes of coloured light made it difficult to see who was in front of me. This was both a good and a bad thing. Good, because that most likely meant people couldn't see who was hiding inside the too-large hoodie that hung from my body. Bad, because I couldn't find Marty anywhere.

At least I hadn't run into Trent yet. I guessed he was waiting to make a fashionably late entrance.

Arms, legs and bodies moved rhythmically to the deafening music. I was about to give up and go home. I wasn't sure I had the courage to ask Jemma to dance with me. For all I knew, she wasn't here anyway.

As I eyed the exit, something from across the dance floor caught my eye. The flashing lights reflecting off its four shiny steel studs. Two red stripes moving to the beat. I couldn't believe it: it was the jacket from the shop. And inside that jacket was Marty, his face gleaming with confidence. A circle had gathered around him. Students were clapping and cheering as Marty threw his fist into the air when the song finished. People walked in and gave him high-fives. It had finally happened; Marty had become a popular kid.

As the next song began, the crowd of students began to dance away. I approached Marty, shock all over my face. Marty's eyes lit up when he saw me.

'You made it!' he exclaimed, and began doing the robot.

'What do you think you're doing?' I yelled against the music.

'Dancing, what does it look like?' Marty replied as he spun around.

I stood there in disbelief.

'You stole the jacket.'

'Borrowed,' he corrected as he did the sprinkler in my direction. 'I'm going to take it back tomorrow.'

I was about to give him a lecture when I saw her. Jemma Arrows, dressed in a beautiful blue dress, dancing by herself.

I looked at Marty and the stolen jacket. Then I looked back at Jemma. I shook my head at Marty and made my way across the dance floor.

I could feel the butterflies in my gut bouncing to the bass of the song. I could feel my knees shaking as I approached. Then Jemma noticed me and smiled. That's when I knew there was no turning back.

I started to bop awkwardly closer to her. My giant hoodie felt like it was dragging along the ground.

'Hi, Paddy,' she called out, continuing to dance.

'Hi!' I called back, louder than I expected. I was incredibly nervous. After dreaming about this moment the entire school year, I had finally found the courage to make it to a disco and dance with Jemma. The problem was, I had no idea how to dance.

I started bobbing my knees and waving my hands towards the floor. I tried to incorporate a dance move that allowed me to pull my hoodie sleeves back up to my wrist. I looked like a broken marionette doll. But Jemma didn't seem to mind.

'I like your moves,' she said, showing me her amazing smile.

I smiled back. The butterflies in my stomach disappeared. I began to feel more confident and move more freely.

That's when I was bumped hard from behind. I spun around to meet Marty's terrified expression. One of his arms was pointing out to the side. The other was bent with his hand planted against his head. He was frozen in mid-sprinkler.

'Help me!' he said, loud enough for only me to hear. 'Something terrible is happening. I can't move!'

I looked over at Jemma. She continued to smile and dance. I turned back to Marty. His arms locked in place. His face pleading.

I turned to Jemma.

'Excuse me for a minute.'

Before Jemma could respond, I grabbed Marty by the bottom of the jacket and quickly pulled him into the boys' toilets.

'What is going on?' I asked as I directed Marty into one of the cubicles and locked the door. Marty sat down. His arms were still frozen in mid-sprinkler. 'Is this some sort of joke?'

'I'm freaking out!' Marty whispered above the low thud of the music outside. 'I can't move my arms.'

I grabbed Marty's elbow and tried to pull it down, but it wouldn't budge. I pulled back his jacket sleeve to see if he had some sort of stick under his arm. I wanted to see if he was playing a trick on me.

That's when I saw it. Not a stick. Just Marty's arm. It was shiny and smooth. I grabbed his wrist to find it cold and hard. Like plastic.

Just Marty's ARM. It was SHINY & smooth

And that's when it hit me.

'Oh no,' I whispered as I let go of his wrist and stumbled back.

'What?' Marty choked, his eyes desperate for an answer. 'What is it?'

I looked him up and down before delivering the news.

'You're turning into a mannequin.'

Marty began to freak out. He tried to stand, but his legs had also frozen stiff.

'HOW? WHY?' He stared at his arms and legs. 'What is happening?'

'Have you eaten something strange?' I asked, reaching for an explanation. 'Or danced too much?'

'Danced too much?' Marty screamed back at me. 'There's no such thing!'

He leaned against the wall. The buttons on his jacket gleamed in the bathroom's fluorescent lights.

And then it all clicked.

'The jacket!' I cried. 'The jacket is **cursed!**'

Marty looked down. His mouth dropped open.

'You're right,' he said. 'I've been cursed for stealing the jacket from the mannequin. And now I'm turning into one!' His eyes grew wide. 'Get this off me!' he exclaimed. 'Hurry!'

I pulled down the jacket's zipper and tried to force it off his body. But it was no use. Marty's arms were stuck solid in sprinkler pose. There was no way of getting it off.

'It's no use,' Marty conceded as I stopped tugging at the jacket.

There was a moment of silence as I looked around. There had to be a way to fix this. I clicked my fingers when I found the answer.

'It's Friday,' I announced, 'which means late-night shopping. We have time to get it back before it's too late.'

'But I'm stuck,' Marty moaned, looking down at his legs. 'I can't walk.'

I was already one step ahead.

The squeak of the wheels was terrible. Thankfully, it was masked by the deafening beat of the school disco. Although we were in a hurry, I had to move cautiously as I balanced Marty on top of the bucket. The handle of the mop rattled against the inside of the arm locked against the side of his head. I'm sure it was far from comfortable for Marty, but it was our only hope.

So we didn't draw too much attention to

ourselves, I hid Marty and his shiny plastic body behind my oversized hoodie and put on the pair of overalls and the legionnaire's hat that hung behind the mop and bucket back in the school bathroom. Hopefully, it was enough to hide the two terrified twelve-year-olds who were about to attempt to return a stolen jacket.

Fortunately, the shopping mall was only a couple of blocks from the school. The echo of the squeaking wheels provided a not-so-grand entrance as we walked through the doors. Shoppers from all around looked in our direction, the noise obviously disturbing their retail experience.

'We're dead meat,' Marty croaked from behind the hoodie. 'There's no way we can pull this off.'

I stopped out the front of Kazaar Clothing. Without the squeak of the bucket, the world seemed silent.

I took a deep breath.

'Here goes nothing.'

The squeak of the bucket returned as we

made our way into the shop. I wanted to get there as quickly as I could, but the faster I pushed the mop and bucket, the louder the squeak echoed through the shop.

My hands were sweaty. I realised I was tiptoeing through the aisles. I felt like I was holding my breath. I needed to get to the mannequin as quickly as possible.

I turned the corner and entered the boys' clothing section. Then I stopped dead. The mannequin that once wore the jacket was gone. It no longer stood on the display platform. I didn't know what to do.

'HEY!'

A stern voice from behind me made my heart stop. I slowly turned around to see a lady standing with her hands on her hips. Her 'Store Manager' badge swung from the lanyard around her neck.

'What exactly do you think you are doing?'

I couldn't speak. I couldn't move. We were goners.

The store manager walked closer. She

looked down at the giant lump that was hidden behind the oversized hoodie.

'What do we have under there?' Her voice was both curious and cautious.

'It's – it's…' I stammered.

But before I could say anything else, she bent down and unzipped the hoodie. I closed my eyes and waited for her to call out to security. Waited to be accused as a shoplifter.

'Ah,' she began, her voice now warmer. 'I was wondering when this was going to arrive.'

I opened my eyes and looked down. Sitting on top of the bucket, its arm wrapped around the mop, was a mannequin. A mannequin wearing the two-striped leather jacket. Nothing about the mannequin resembled Marty. We were too late; Marty was gone.

'This is perfect,' the manager continued. 'It looks very *street*, as they say. This is going straight to the storefront. Thank you.'

In stunned disbelief, I didn't even notice her take the mop handle away from me. I watched as she pushed the mannequin towards the front of the shop. I couldn't believe what had just happened. Marty had transformed into a mannequin. Gone. Forever. All for stealing a stupid leather jacket.

With my head hanging low, I finally walked out of the shop. I stood staring at the front display window and watched as the store manager sat Marty down on a podium. His arms and legs were now able to be moved but only as awkwardly as those of a mannequin.

When she walked away, I stepped forward and put my hands on the glass.

'I'm so sorry,' I whispered.

And then the mannequin blinked. I almost jumped out of my overalls.

'Marty!' I cried. **'YOU'RE STILL ALIVE!'**

A shadow approached from the inside. I quickly jumped back and hid behind a rubbish bin in the middle of the mall. Just in time to see another person enter the front display. His blond streak gleaming against the shop lights. His eyes locked on the leather jacket. I watched, wide-eyed, as Trent Rowe neared the mannequin. He looked left and right before forcing the jacket from Marty's body. I gasped in shock as he bundled it under his shirt and casually walked out of the shop. Trent Rowe had stolen the jacket.

As Trent strolled away down the mall, I looked back at Marty. His eyes were wide, pleading for me to help. It was now or never.

I ran back inside and picked Marty up. I threw him over my shoulders and ran out of the store. Every shopper stopped and stared. I didn't blame them; it's not every day you see a kid in overalls and a legionnaire's hat sprinting through the mall piggybacking a mannequin.

My legs burned. My heart raced. But I didn't stop. I wanted to be as far away from the mall as possible.

I had no idea whether or not it was too late. Whether or not Marty was still inside the mannequin.

We were a block away from the school when

I felt Marty's arm move and grip my shoulders. I stopped and felt him slip down to the road. My legs gave way and I collapsed to the ground.

'Well, that didn't tickle,' Marty said as he gingerly stood up.

He was back. Marty had beaten the curse of the jacket.

I quickly jumped up and helped him regain his balance.

'Are you okay?' I asked.

Marty turned and looked towards the mall.

'Trent Rowe has poor taste.'

We looked at each other and laughed hysterically. If only Trent knew.

The sound of music could be heard in the distance.

'Come on,' Marty said. 'You still have time for that dance with Jemma.'

We both smiled and made our way back to the school disco.

I did finally get to dance with Jemma for

a whole twenty-five seconds before the last song of the night finished. It was worth it. I promised her I would dance for a full minute at the next disco.

What made the disco even better was that it remained Trent-free. He never showed. And I'm pretty sure I know why.

Trent wasn't at school the following Monday. Or for the rest of the week, in fact.

The school seemed to be a different place. A place where you could be comfortable wearing two-star shoes or oversized shirts. It didn't matter. It was no longer a big deal.

On Friday night, Mum dragged us back to the shops to find Dad a birthday present. Even though I was well hidden behind the legionnaire's hat, I still felt a little nervous.

'What do you reckon, kids?' Mum asked as we made our way towards CrazyMart.

'What about some new undies?' Troy suggested as he swung on the side of the trolley to the point where it could almost tip over. 'Or a new toothbrush?'

'Hmm, what about this?' Mum called, stopping a clothes rack outside Kazaar Clothing.

Mum played with the zipper. She cleaned the four steel studs. She ran her fingers down the two red stripes. 'He is due for a new jacket.'

'Ew, gross,' Nina replied as she took a rare

moment to look up from her phone. 'That jacket is so last winter.'

'Fair enough then.' Mum moved away from the jacket, grabbed the trolley and made a beeline for CrazyMart with Nina and Troy in toe.

I stood there looking at the cursed jacket. It didn't look comfortable on the mannequin. A little too tight. And the red stripes lost their glamour against the blond streak in the mannequin's dark hair.

I smiled before joining my family in finding the daggiest gift possible.

Trent did return to school the following week. But not the Trent we once knew. Instead of a blond streak through his hair, he arrived with a clean-cut look. And to match his new hairdo, he brought along a new positive attitude. He even offered an apple to Marty when Marty had forgotten his lunch. It was incredible.

But not as incredible as the new student who had started at Top Hill Primary. He was tall and had bright blue eyes. His gleaming smile revealed a row of perfect white teeth. He was funny and kind to all the students. He made everyone feel good about themselves. He was perfect.

Everyone was curious though about the V-shaped scar on his cheek.

The Black-Toothed Bandit

I could smell it straight away. That distinct sour odour. Like the smell you get when you open the milk to realise it's been out of date for weeks. Or the stink of the garbage bin on New Year's Eve after the summer heat has fermented Christmas Day's prawn shells. Combine those two smells and multiply it by a hundred. That's what lingered in my nostrils.

Dad turned onto Daffodil Drive. There was nothing daffodil about it. It should've been called Decomposing Drive. All the same, we were almost there.

By 'there', you might be thinking the transfer station, or as Dad likes to call it, the tip. Or maybe you're thinking we were approaching swamplands with ibises, pigeons and other dirty birds. No, this was worse. We were approaching my uncle's house.

Keith Pimble. Or as Mum liked to call him, **the HOARDER**.

'He's a collector,' Dad would always argue. Deep down I'm sure he knew Mum was right.

Uncle Keith collected everything. I'm not just talking about things with value, like porcelain, books, stamps and paintings. He collected ev-er-y-thing. Old newspapers, egg cartons, sauce bottles, fruit stickers, shoelaces, worn tyres, broken fence panelling. All the stuff most people throw out. Our garbage was his treasure.

The only limit to what he collected was how much he could fit on his property. From what I could see ahead of me, he had

EGG CARTONS

OLD NEWSPAPERS

TOP DOG IN TOP HILL

SAUCE BOTTLES

FRUIT STICKERS

SHOELACES

FENCE PANELLING

WORN TYRES

TREASURE

obviously reached his boundary and was now
building up towards the sky.

As we pulled up on the street outside,
I realised I couldn't see the house. It was
completely covered in rubbish, a yellow
fog lingering above it. A tunnel had been

burrowed out of the mass of refuse that
I assumed led to the front door.

I was wrong about one thing: there were
ibises and pigeons. They browsed among the
piles of old wrappers, bottles and papers. It
was putrid.

'Are you sure about this, Andrew?' Mum
asked, leaning into the back seat and
covering Bella's nose with a tissue. 'Does he
not have someone else?'

'I'm Keith's brother, sweetheart,' Dad said.
'He'll have nowhere else to stay.'

You see, Uncle Keith was about to be kicked
out of his home. All the neighbours had

complained about the mess and smell. On top of this, Uncle Keith had lost his job at the car dealership, so he could no longer afford it. We had driven up here to tell him he could move into our place. Mum wasn't very thrilled about this, and neither was I.

But Dad would always say, 'You do for family,' and we couldn't argue with that. Nina and Troy were smart. They had both organised sleepovers, knowing that today would be a disaster. I hadn't thought quickly enough. So here I was with Dad, Mum and Bella out the front of the most disgusting house in Australia.

We got out of the car and made our way up the tunnel of filth, our only light the holes that had been gnawed out by rats and scavenging birds. We made it to the front door and knocked softly, just in case the tunnel decided to collapse.

We could hear someone rummaging through the house, possibly looking for the door. Glass bottles, tins and papers being disturbed.

Then the door opened.

Standing there, in the same light brown suit that he had been wearing since the early 1970s, was Uncle Keith. He wore his black, greasy hair slicked to one side, clearly hoping to hide all that he had lost on top. His long, thick sideburns were slightly grey. His eyebrows were the same colour but were beginning to take on a life of their own as they sprouted in every direction.

UNCLE KEITH

'Well, well, well.' He chuckled, revealing a not-so-gleaming set of yellow teeth. A similar yellow to his shirt. 'It's about time you got here.'

Dad held out his hand, but Uncle Keith leaned in and gave Dad a big hug. I could see by Dad's face that he was holding his breath.

Mum faked a cough and held Bella tight in her arms when Uncle Keith let go of Dad.

'Sorry Keith, I have a bad cold. Better not come too close.'

Uncle Keith chuckled again before wrapping his arms around Mum. Poor Bella's cheek was squished up against his smelly shirt.

'I'm sure it's nothing too bad,' he insisted, squeezing Mum tighter. 'Besides, I'm so thankful you came.'

'It's...lovely...up here,' Dad lied, looking around at the rubbish-stained walls.

Uncle Keith let go of Mum. Her eyes were almost popping out of her head. Bella looked up at Mum in shock.

He reached over and squeezed my cheeks.

His fingers felt like they were covered in grease.

'I see you've lost the cheeks, Paddy.'

All I could do was let out a nervous chuckle.

'Come on in.' Uncle Keith turned around and led the way inside. He had made a trail through the knee-high debris. I scrubbed my cheek with my shirt. Mum looked at Dad in disgust. Dad could only shrug his shoulders.

We were led to what must have been the dining room, as a table and four chairs rose out of the junk. Mum, Dad and Keith sat down at the table. Mum perched Bella on the table as far away as possible from any of the rubbish.

Uncle Keith motioned to the back of the house.

'Zoe's back there, mate.'

My eyes widened. Zoe Pimble was here. The one and only Zoe Pimble.

Although her father was a little weird, Zoe Pimble was a **GENIUS**. Literally. Zoe had been away for the past two years at a top-secret science camp in China. She was invited after she created a washing detergent that, after one wash, made clothes remain clean and ironed for the rest of their existence.

But now Zoe Pimble was back in Alpine Park.

'Is that you, Paddy?' Zoe stuck her head out from her bedroom. She still had the same bob cut as the last time I saw her.

'Hi, Zoe,' I responded, still in shock.

'Come in here.' She waved me over. Her voice was full of excitement. **'I've got to show you something.'**

I pulled myself through the rubbish and made my way to Zoe's room.

'Quick, close the door,' Zoe said.

Surprisingly, her room was spotless. Not a piece of rubbish in sight. Her bed was made, her carpeted floor freshly vacuumed. Even her books on the shelf had been sorted in size order. I was impressed.

'You've come just in time,' Zoe said as she sat at her desk. In front of her were what looked like plans. A long list of letters and numbers and arrows and lines. None of it made sense to me.

'What is that?' I asked.

Zoe smiled, baring her black tooth, a reminder of the time she tried to create a toothpaste that never wore off. Her black tooth was the test tooth. The toothpaste had had the reverse effect.

She SMILED ✦✦

...baring her BLACK TOOTH.

Zoe opened her top drawer and pulled out an old soft drink can.

'What is this?' she asked, pointing to the can.

'Is this a JOKE?' I replied.

'No, seriously, what is it?'

'It's a can, Zoe,' I said, confused. 'Are you all right?'

Zoe opened her bottom drawer, pulled out a small yellow container and placed it on her desk.

'This is going to change everything,' she announced as she put on a rubber glove. 'This is going to solve all our problems.'

Zoe carefully opened the container. Inside was what looked like purple sand. Using a pair of tweezers, she pinched a tiny sample of the purple grains from the container and placed them on top of the can. Then, using an eye-dropper, she took some water out of her bottle.

'Are you ready for this?' Her black tooth stared back at me as she smirked.

'Um, I guess,' I replied.

Zoe hung the eye-dropper over the top of the can. She gently squeezed it until one droplet fell on to the sand.

An amazing sight met my eyes. A plume

of purple smoke rose, consuming the can. Flashes of purple electricity from inside the cloud lit up the room. A low rumbling sound like distant thunder stirred within.

And then it stopped. I had to blink my eyes a few times to adjust back to the room. I felt like I had just stared into the flash of a camera. Zoe was waving her hands in the air, clearing the remnants of the smoke.

As my normal sight returned, I noticed the can had disappeared. Instead, sitting in its place sat a five-dollar note.

I couldn't believe what I was seeing. Neither could Zoe. Our eyes were wide with excitement.

'**It worked!**' she yelled.

'What is it?'

Zoe picked up the purple powder.

'This substance will turn any piece of rubbish into a five-dollar note.' Zoe ran over to her door and opened it up. The knee-high garbage collapsed into her room. 'And I have enough to transform every piece in this house.'

I couldn't believe what I was hearing.

'You mean you can turn all of this junk into money?'

Zoe nodded.

'That's amazing! You'll be rich!'

Suddenly, a popping sound came from underneath Zoe's bed.

'There is one problem,' she said.

The popping sound grew louder, more

frequent. A noise like popcorn in a pan. That's when Zoe's bed started to rise as a mountain of rubbish began to grow beneath it. The popping continued for a few more seconds, and when it stopped Zoe's bed was up against the ceiling. Refuse covered the floor.

I looked over at her.

'As you can see, it wears off after a couple of hours.' She walked over and picked up the five-dollar note on her table. 'But that's enough time.'

'Enough time for what?' I asked.

Zoe handed me the five-dollar note.

'I have a plan, Paddy,' she said. 'But I need your help.'

Zoe led the way out of her bedroom window. The backyard was not much different to the front. However, instead of tunnels, the rubbish was built up like a labyrinth, with various paths leading in different directions.

We stopped beside an old rusty BMX bike.

Attached to it was a train of old shopping trolleys. I counted ten of them.

'All right, I'll start loading these ones,' Zoe said. 'You start with the others.'

She directed me around the corner. There I saw another ten trolleys lined up. But they weren't attached to a BMX bike. No, these were attached to a tiny tricycle.

'You're not serious, are you?' I called out. 'That thing wouldn't pull a bag of feathers!'

'Trust me, I've tested it,' Zoe said as she started filling her trolleys with rubbish. 'Quick, we don't have much time.'

I shook my head and started throwing all sorts of junk into the trolleys. Papers, bottles, egg cartons, car parts, cups, pencils, cutlery, clothes, toys. You get the picture.

It took about half an hour to fill all twenty trolleys. I felt disgusting, like I had just jumped headfirst into a wheelie bin. My grey shirt was as brown as the ground. My hands looked like I had been building sandcastles out of oil. And don't get me started on the smell.

'Great.' Zoe smiled, her black tooth matching her once-cream shorts.

'Now for a little magic.'

She pulled out the rubber glove and put it back on. Then she took the container of purple sand from her pocket.

'You ready?' Zoe's voice was shaky, as though all her former confidence had disappeared.

I nodded. Zoe started sprinkling the purple powder onto each of the twenty trolleys. Once done, she walked over to the hose and

turned it on. She aimed it at the ground and gave me a look of confirmation.

I closed my eyes as Zoe sprayed the trolleys. The backyard lit up with flashes of purple. Giant plumes of lilac smoke covered the trolleys. There was a boom and rumble, like an approaching storm.

Zoe ran over and turned off the tap. She shielded her eyes as the lightning continued to flicker. And with one last clap of thunder, everything stopped.

The smoke began to disappear and the trolleys came into view. Zoe and I gasped.

Each of the twenty trolleys held a pile of five-dollar notes. There were thousands of them.

YOU DID IT! YOU'RE RICH!

'Yes!' I screamed. 'You did it! You're rich!'

Zoe held up her dirty rubber-gloved finger, silencing me.

'It's not over yet,' she explained. 'We need to keep filling these until they're full of notes, then get to the bank.' She looked at her watch. 'And we need to hurry.'

We didn't waste any time. We continued to fill the trolleys with rubbish and sprinkle the magic sand until we had all twenty of them filled to the brim with five-dollar notes.

Finally, with a nod of approval, Zoe ran to the BMX bike. I looked over at the tricycle. There was no time to argue.

I jumped on the tricycle and started to pedal. Surprisingly, I began to move. It was stronger than I expected.

Zoe pushed past me to lead the way through the labyrinth. We turned left then right and right again as we pedalled our way out of the maze of rubbish.

Finally, we made it out of the junkyard and began our journey to the centre of town.

People couldn't believe what they were seeing. Two bikes pulling twenty shopping trolleys down the main street. Twenty shopping trolleys holding mountains of five-dollar notes. We didn't have time to explain.

We made it to the entrance of the bank. I thought we were going to stop but just as a customer walked out, Zoe began pedalling hard, desperate to make it inside before the automatic doors closed. I had no choice but to follow.

People started screaming as the roar of the trolleys broke the calming silence inside the bank. Zoe came to an abrupt halt in the

middle of the floor.
I crashed into her,
causing a deafening
bang.

An overweight
man in a suit
came storming
towards us.

His 'Manager' badge swung on his blue tie.

'What is going on here?' he demanded,
his face red and his eyes surveying the
damage.

Zoe jumped off her bike and held out her
hand.

'Hi, Mr Williams, I'm Zoe Pimble, daughter
of Keith Pimble.'

Mr Williams's eyes locked on the trolleys
full of money, wide in both disbelief and
anger.

'What is this?' he asked.

'I've come to pay off Dad's house.'

Mr Williams turned to Zoe, who was still
holding her hand out, her black-toothed smile

spread across her face. He slowly took the hand and gave it a shake.

'Let me get my counters.'

We watched as Mr Williams poured the notes from each trolley into the counting machine. It was taking forever. Every now and then Zoe and I would look nervously at the clock, watching each precious minute tick by.

'Well, that's halfway,' Mr Williams announced as he moved on to my trolleys. 'But it seems you'll have more than enough to pay off the loan.'

Zoe approached him. 'Well, if that is the case, Mr Williams, do you mind if we get your signature now? We're in a bit of a hurry.'

'Shouldn't we wait to see how much we have here first?' Mr Williams asked.

Zoe's eyes flicked between Mr Williams and the clock.

'You said there's more than enough. You

can keep the rest.' She gave a small nervous laugh. 'Call it a bonus if you want.'

Mr Williams chuckled.

'Well, what a lovely gesture.' He stood up and clicked his fingers towards a younger employee. 'Mr Limon is getting your papers right now.'

Zoe looked at me and smiled. I returned a wink. She had pulled it off.

That's when we heard it. A single **POP**. Then another. And another. Mr Williams started looking around.

'What was that?' he asked.

The popping sound became more frequent. I looked at Zoe. Zoe looked at me.

'Run!' I screamed, breaking into a sprint.

'Sorry, Mr Williams,' Zoe called as she dashed for the door.

The popping sound began to grow louder as we ran outside.

We bolted as fast as we could down the main street. Behind us, people were running from the bank, screaming. We paused to look.

The popping grew louder as the automatic doors opened and rubbish began to spew out onto the footpath. Tins and paper and bottles and wrappers. Rolling out of the bank like the flow of a river.

'Zoe Pimble!' Mr Williams screamed as he stumbled out, his suit now covered in dirt and grime, his white shirt stained brown.

Zoe and I looked at each other before sprinting towards the house.

In mid-run, Zoe turned towards me, her fingers pinched together.

'I was this close!' she said through gritted teeth. 'Next time, Paddy, it will be perfect.'

All I could do was give an anxious nod.

★ ★ ★

I found out the next week that Zoe was made to clean up the bank. I felt sorry for her. She was just trying to do something right for Uncle Keith.

Almost a month after that, Dad came home with a giant smile spread across his face.

'It's a miracle!' he said. 'Keith must have won the lottery. The bank let him keep the house!'

Mum was super excited. Nina started dancing with Bella in the lounge room. Troy and I gave each other a high-five. Uncle Keith wouldn't have to stay with us. Mum gave Dad a giant hug. Everything worked out after all.

'That'll be four dollars twenty.'

I gave the shopkeeper my ten-dollar note.

As she opened the till I couldn't help but wonder if Zoe had something to do with her dad's new fortune. If she had somehow tricked everyone. I came to the conclusion that it would be impossible to get away with it twice.

'That's five dollars eighty change.'

'Thank you.'

I dropped the coins into my pocket as I left the shop. Just when I was about to put the five-dollar note in my wallet, something caught my attention. Something oddly familiar.

I held the note up to the sun. That's when I saw the Queen's smile. It was different somehow – it revealed her teeth. And among those teeth was an all-too-familiar black one. The mark of the Black-Toothed Bandit.

I laughed all the way home.

Adam France lives in Brisbane where he works as a primary school teacher. When he's not moulding young minds in the classroom, Adam is rocking out on guitar, throwing paint on canvases and writing twisted stories for kids. All this while juggling family life with his partner, Bree, and six-year-old daughter, Frankie.

Zahra Zainal is a Melbourne-based illustrator and graphic recorder. After a few short stints in the world of teaching and greeting cards, she found herself scribbling her way through life as a full-time illustrator. Some of her favourite moments as an illustrator include: a group exhibition in her backyard, and having her artwork covering a Melbourne tram. She loves libraries, coffee and reality talent shows.
Zahrazainal.com